Cambridge Experien

Level 3

Series editor: Nicholas Tims

The Mind Map

David Morrison

CAMBRIDGE
UNIVERSITY PRESS

CAMBRIDGE
UNIVERSITY PRESS

University Printing House, Cambridge CB2 8BS, United Kingdom

One Liberty Plaza, 20th Floor, New York, NY 10006, USA

477 Williamstown Road, Port Melbourne, VIC 3207, Australia

4843/24, 2nd Floor, Ansari Road, Daryaganj, Delhi – 110002, India

79 Anson Road, #06–04/06, Singapore 079906

José Abascal 56, 1° – 28003 Madrid, Spain

Cambridge University Press is part of the University of Cambridge.

It furthers the University's mission by disseminating knowledge in the pursuit of education, learning and research at the highest international levels of excellence.

www.cambridge.org
Information on this title: www.cambridge.org9788483235379

First published 2009
20 19 18 17 16 15 14 13 12 11 10 9
Printed in Spain by GraphyCems

ISBN 978-84-832-3537-9 Paperback; legal deposit: S.936-2009

No character in this work is based on any person living or dead. Any resemblance to an actual person or situation is purely accidental.

Illustrations by Ricardo Robles

Audio recording by BraveArts, S.L.

Exercises by Peter McDonnell

Contents

People in the story

Lucho Valdez: a fifteen-year-old boy
Eva Villa: Lucho's classmate
Mr Parra: the history teacher at Lucho's school
Pablo Silva: another of Lucho's classmates
Mario: a young man; he works in Salvador's antique shop
Salvador Lana: the owner of an antique shop
the chief: the leader of the Kogi tribe

BEFORE YOU READ

1 Look at the cover and the pictures in the first chapter. Answer the questions.

1 Where is the story set?

....

2 What animals are there in the story?

....

Chapter 1

Homework

Lucho Valdez looked at the little yellow bird singing happily in a tree on the other side of the classroom window.

'It's almost as beautiful as Eva Villa,' he thought to himself.

Eva was sitting at the front of the class. Lucho could only see the back of her head, but he knew she was listening to every word their history teacher, Mr Parra, was saying.

'The problem is that I don't know anything about her,' Lucho said to himself. 'I don't know what she does after school. I don't know if she likes going to the cinema, if she likes pizza, or if she has a boyfriend. I don't even know where she lives in Santa Marta! And I certainly don't know what she thinks about me!'

'And what do you think, Lucho?'

Lucho's name woke him from his daydream.

'Did you even hear my question, Lucho?' asked Mr Parra.

The students at the front of the class turned round to watch the show. They were all smiling. Eva Villa had turned to watch too, but she wasn't smiling. For a moment Eva looked straight into Lucho's dark, sad eyes and he could feel his face turning bright[1] red. Then she turned back to the front and said something to the girl sitting next to her. The girl laughed.

Mr Parra walked towards Lucho's desk. Lucho liked Mr Parra, although he didn't like history class. There was too much information to remember.

'Maybe you could tell us what I have been talking about for the last twenty minutes, Lucho, while you were looking out of the window,' said Mr Parra.

Lucho's heart felt heavy. He had no idea what to say. He looked down at his history textbook. The page was about 'The stolen past' and there was a photograph of a gold object[2] that looked very old. Next he looked quickly at the board and saw one of Mr Parra's favourite things: a mind map. Every time they had to write about something for homework, Mr Parra asked them to make a mind map.

The mind map had four empty circles joined by four lines to a bigger circle in the centre. In the centre circle Mr Parra had written the word 'guaca'. Lucho tried to remember where he had heard the word before.

They were all waiting. Lucho looked out the window for a second and saw the little yellow bird. Yes, that was it! *Guaca* was a word that his grandmother had used, but what did it mean? The class was still waiting for him to speak. Suddenly he heard the little yellow bird singing in the tree outside and he opened his mouth.

'We were talking about *guaca*, sir,' he answered.

'And what is *guaca*, Lucho?' Mr Parra asked.

'*Guaca* means "special object". An antique[3] object that was made by South American tribes,[4] usually from gold, sir.'

Mr Parra looked surprised. He hadn't expected Lucho to know the answer. Lucho felt strange. He had no idea where the words were coming from.

'The people who lived here in Colombia, before Christopher Columbus and the Spanish arrived, made lots of gold *guaca*. But many years later collectors[5] all over the world became very interested in these objects and took the *guaca* out of Colombia.'

The girl next to Eva turned to look at Lucho again. The rest of Lucho's classmates had lost interest. Lucho felt better, but Mr Parra hadn't finished with him yet.

'That's correct, Lucho,' said Mr Parra. 'And what is today's homework?'

Homework? Lucho hadn't heard Mr Parra talk about homework. He looked at the mind map on the blackboard again. Outside, the bird had stopped singing.

'I'm not sure, sir,' Lucho said quietly. He felt stupid. 'Is it something about *guaca*?'

His classmates laughed. Mr Parra turned to another student in the class.

'Can you help us, Pablo?'

Pablo Silva was every teacher's favourite student. He always knew the answer to every question. Some people didn't like him and laughed at his old-fashioned glasses, but Lucho thought he was OK and he sometimes helped Lucho with his homework when he hadn't listened in class.

'We have to write four hundred words by next Thursday about why *guaca* should be returned to Colombia, sir,' Pablo answered. 'But first we have to find out some information and organise it into a mind map like the one on the board.'

'That's correct, Pablo. Thank you. Give me your mind maps on Monday, and …'

When they heard the bell for end of class, everybody started putting their things in their bags.

'Wait a minute, wait a minute!' shouted Mr Parra.

Mr Parra made a loud noise with his ruler. Lucho saw the little yellow bird fly into the air when it heard the noise.

'I'll check your mind maps in class on Monday. Remember, they are as important as the written work!'

Lucho put his books into his bag and walked towards the classroom door with the rest of the class.

'We can do this really quickly.'

The voice was Eva Villa's. Lucho turned and saw that she was standing behind him waiting to leave the class.

'Sorry?' he said.

Lucho looked at Eva's lovely dark brown eyes and her long black hair. Unfortunately, he turned red again.

'I said that we can do this really quickly. We can do the mind map together tomorrow in the library. That way we won't have to meet this weekend,' Eva continued.

She could see that Lucho didn't understand.

'Don't worry, you were probably asleep!' she joked.

'Mr Parra said we had to do the homework in pairs. I have to work with you,' she explained patiently. 'It's Friday tomorrow so we have a free hour after English class. We can use the Internet in the library.'

Lucho wanted to shout with happiness. He was going to spend an hour in the library with Eva Villa. Eva Villa!

'Um, yes, OK,' Lucho replied. 'Tomorrow morning, in the library, after English class.'

He had tried to sound cool but, when he walked out of the classroom, he could feel his heart beating hard in his chest.

LOOKING BACK

● ●

1 Check your answers to *Before you read* on page 4.

ACTIVITIES

● ●

2 Are the sentences true (*T*) or false (*F*)?

1 Mr Parra is Lucho's geography teacher. ☐F☐
2 Eva lives in a town called Santa Marta. ☐
3 A mind map has got lines and circles. ☐
4 *Guaca* is the name of gold objects from North America. ☐
5 Lucho lives in Colombia. ☐
6 All the teachers like Pablo Silva. ☐
7 Mr Parra says that mind maps are not important. ☐
8 Lucho and Pablo are going to do their homework together. ☐
9 Lucho and Eva are going to meet in the library the next day. ☐

3 <u>Underline</u> the correct words in each sentence.

1 Lucho *is* / <u>*isn't*</u> listening to his teacher.
2 Lucho knows *a lot* / *very little* about Eva.
3 Lucho likes *Mr Parra* / *history*.
4 There *is* / *isn't* a lot of *guaca* in Colombia now.
5 The students have to do their mind maps *before* / *after* they do their written work.
6 The students have to do their mind maps for *Monday* / *Thursday*.
7 Lucho and Eva are going to do their homework *on Friday* / *at the weekend*.
8 Eva *thinks* / *doesn't think* that they can do the homework quickly.
9 Lucho *feels* / *doesn't feel* nervous at the end of Chapter 1.

10

4 What do the underlined words refer to in these lines from the text?

1 'It's almost as beautiful as Eva Villa.' (page 5) *the yellow bird*

2 Lucho could only see the back of her head. (page 5)
....

3 They were all smiling. (page 6) ....

4 He had no idea what to say. (page 7) ....

5 He always knew the answer to every question. (page 8)
....

6 'We can do this really quickly.' (page 8) ....

7 'I have to work with you.' (page 9) ....

5 Answer the questions.

1 What is Lucho looking at at the beginning of the story?
....

2 Why doesn't Lucho like history?
....

3 Who took the *guaca* out of Colombia?
....

4 What is the homework for Thursday?
....

LOOKING FORWARD

6 Tick (✓) what you think happens in the next two chapters.

1 Lucho talks to his mother about *guaca*. ☐

2 Lucho and Eva find a piece of *guaca*. ☐

Chapter 2

Guaca

Lucho cycled home after school, but he felt like he was flying. Before he opened the door to the flat where he and his mother lived, he could smell the delicious cheese *arepa* she had made for him.

'How was your day?' his mother asked.

'Fine, Mum. Just fine,' he replied.

He left his bag on the sofa and went into the bathroom to wash his hands.

He looked at himself in the mirror. He needed a haircut, but it was not going to be possible to go to the hairdresser's before his meeting with Eva the next day. He would go on Saturday. He dried his hands and went back into the living room.

'Did you work hard at school today, Lucho?' his mother asked.

'Yes, Mum. I always work hard,' he answered smiling.

'So why don't you pass your exams?'

His mother asked him this question at least once a week.

'I will pass my exams this time, Mum, I promise,' Lucho answered.

He took a bite of the *arepa*. The soft, warm cheese escaped from inside the corn bread onto his fingers. Delicious!

'Gran used to talk about *guaca*, didn't she, Mum?' Lucho asked.

'Sometimes she did, yes, Lucho.' His mother looked at him strangely then she continued. 'She used to say that Colombia would be rich if all its *guaca* was returned. Why do you ask?'

'Um …' he thought about telling his mum about Eva but decided not to. 'I have to do some written work about it for history class, with a partner.'

'I see.' Lucho's mum smiled as she spoke. 'With a partner. Interesting …'

Lucho turned red for the third time that day. He stood up and took his empty plate into the kitchen. While he was washing the plate, a little yellow bird landed just outside the window. It looked like the same yellow bird that he had seen outside the history classroom.

'Hello,' said Lucho. 'Are you following me?'

The bird looked at Lucho and then flew onto the line where his mother dried their clothes. Then it flew up into the blue sky.

When he went back into the living room, his mother was watching television.

'Is this partner a girl, Lucho?' she asked.

'Mum! It's just someone from my history class.'

'I knew it.' His mother was smiling from ear to ear. 'I knew it,' she repeated. 'Is she nice?'

'Mum, please!' Lucho didn't like it when his mother asked him about girls.

'What's her name, Lucho? Is it Eva Villa?' she asked.

Sometimes Lucho's mother seemed to know what was happening in his life before he had told her.

'Yes, Mum, I have to do a mind map with Eva Villa,' he replied.

Lucho's mother worked with Eva's mother. He knew what she was going to say next.

'Eva's a very good student, isn't she, Lucho?' his mother asked.

'Yes, Mum,' replied Lucho.

'And she's very pretty,' his mum continued. 'If you want to be her boyfriend, you will have to study hard.'

'Mum! I do not want to be Eva Villa's boyfriend!'

Lucho was angry now. He stood up and started walking

out of the living room. His mother laughed at him, but in a nice way.

'Sit down, Lucho.' Her voice was serious.

'Let me tell you about Gran and *guaca.*'

Lucho sat down on the sofa again. His mother turned the television off.

'You know your grandmother was a cleaner in an expensive hotel near the port,[6] don't you? Well, a man from the USA – an American – was staying at the hotel for several months. He and your grandmother became good friends. One day the man asked her to help him. He showed her a beautiful gold pendant and asked her to look after it while he went to Bogota for a week to do some business. He said the pendant was a very special piece of *guaca* and that he was going to take it back to its home in the Sierra Nevada mountains when he returned from Bogota. He didn't want to put it in a bank, he said, because he didn't like banks. Your grandmother promised to look after it.'

Lucho felt bad and tried not to look into his mother's eyes. He knew which pendant she was talking about.

'What happened to the American man, Mum?' he asked.

'He never came back to Santa Marta, Lucho. And your grandmother never told me what happened to the pendant.'

There was a photograph of Lucho's grandmother on the living room wall. Lucho looked at it. Her eyes were quick and intelligent, like a bird's.

'Was the American a good man, Mum?' he asked.

'Your grandmother said he was a good man, yes, Lucho.'

Lucho thanked his mother and went into his bedroom. He closed the door behind him and opened the drawer in the table next to his bed. Carefully, he took out a small blue bag from the drawer, opened it and took out the gold pendant the American had given to his grandmother.

The pendant was a perfect circle, like the sun. In its centre was the head of a jaguar. The jaguar was looking straight out at Lucho and was showing its teeth. Above the jaguar's head was a little bird. It looked just like the yellow bird he had seen outside the history class window and then later outside his kitchen window.

Lucho felt bad again. He had never told anybody about the pendant; not even his mother. A few weeks before his grandmother died, she had called him to her room and given him the blue bag.

'Take this, Lucho, and look after it,' she had told him. 'Don't tell anyone about it, not even your mother. Never sell it or give it to anyone or something bad could happen. One day the pendant will ask you to help it to go home.'

It had been a long day and he felt tired. He closed his eyes and thought about Eva. He really liked Eva. Then he had an idea. If he started the mind map, he could show it to her the next day. Then Eva would see that he wasn't lazy. He opened his notebook and used the pendant to draw the first circle of the mind map. He wrote 'guaca' in the circle, and then drew four more circles, two to the left and two to the right, just like Mr Parra's mind map on the board in history class. Next he used a ruler to draw lines between the centre circle and the four other circles. Finally, he opened his history textbook and

started reading about 'stolen gold'. He hoped he would find some more words to write in the other circles, but he could feel his eyes closing again. Ten minutes later he was asleep and dreaming.

In his dream it was a beautiful spring day and he was in history class. Outside a little yellow bird was singing in a tree. Lucho stood up, walked to the front of the class and took Eva's hand. Then he and Eva walked out of the classroom towards the tree where the little yellow bird was singing.

When they were near the tree, the bird flew to another tree and Eva and Lucho followed it. Little by little, they followed the bird out of Santa Marta High School, out of Santa Marta itself, up into the Sierra Nevada mountains and the jungle.

As they climbed higher into the jungle, the trees became taller and the plants larger and stranger. Hand in hand, they followed the bird across a wooden bridge over a noisy river and after a long, long walk they came to a circle of yellow grass. In the centre of the circle was a golden jaguar covered with black spots.[7]

The jaguar looked dangerous. Lucho held Eva in his arms as they watched it climb the tree that the yellow bird was sitting in. When the jaguar was only a few metres away from it, the bird flew up into the bright blue sky. The jaguar jumped towards it but could not catch it. Then black circles appeared on the field of dry yellow grass. To Lucho, the circles looked like a mind map.

'Dinner's ready!'

Lucho woke up suddenly. His mother was calling him. Where was the pendant? When he had fallen asleep, it was on the table next to his bed. Had his mother seen it? He opened the drawer in the table and there was the blue bag with the pendant inside. Lucho was sure he had not put it there.

Chapter 3

The library

The next morning Lucho woke up before his alarm clock rang. For a moment he couldn't remember what day it was. Then he saw his closed notebook on the table beside his bed. It was Friday and he had promised to meet Eva in the library after English class. He jumped out of bed.

His mother had already left for work. Lucho liked it when the house was empty. He quickly ate breakfast then checked his hair in the bathroom mirror.

'You really need a haircut,' he said to himself.

He went back into his bedroom and put his books into his school bag. Then something strange happened: he found himself opening the drawer and taking out the little blue bag with the pendant inside. Something was moving his hand and he couldn't stop it. He felt his hand put the bag in his trouser pocket and when he tried to take it out, his hand would not move.

'That's strange,' he thought. 'Maybe I'm just sleepy.'

Lucho was the first person at English class that Friday morning. He watched Eva as she walked into the class. She always walked so slowly, she always seemed so happy and she always looked so beautiful.

Mrs Murphy, the English teacher, arrived. She liked Lucho because he liked English. If she needed an example and nobody could think of one, she asked him. Today was no different from any other day.

'OK. Listen, please. In our last class we looked at second conditional sentences. Let's practise. If you were an animal, what animal would you be?' Mrs Murphy asked the class.

Nobody answered.

'Lucho, any ideas?'

Without thinking, Lucho answered, 'A jaguar. If I were an animal, I would be a jaguar.'

'Perfect! Thank you, Lucho. Now, can someone else give me an example?'

Lucho finished every activity as quickly as he could: maybe that way the time would pass more quickly, but it didn't. English class passed very slowly that day and all he could think about was his meeting with Eva Villa in the library. Finally, Mrs Murphy told them what their homework was and class was over. Lucho stood up immediately and walked to Eva's desk.

'Hello,' he said.

'Hello,' replied Eva. 'I'll see you in the library in five minutes.'

Lucho walked across the grass between the English classroom and the library building. He was angry with himself because the evening before he had fallen asleep when he was doing the mind map. He had wanted to show Eva that he wasn't as useless as she probably thought. At least he could book a computer for them to use. He walked into the library and stood nervously in front of the librarian.

'I'd like to use the Internet, please,' he told the librarian.

'Can you tell me your name?' the librarian asked.

'Lucho Valdez. I'm going to share the computer with Eva Villa.'

Lucho felt warm inside when he said Eva's name. He looked at his watch. More than five minutes had passed. Maybe Eva wasn't coming. He looked at his watch again and when he looked up, she was standing next to him. He turned red. He hoped she couldn't see that he was nervous.

'Sorry I'm late,' she said.

'That's OK!' replied Lucho. 'I have already asked for a computer.'

'It's number sixteen,' said the librarian.

Lucho sat down next to Eva in front of the computer.

'I started a mind map, but I couldn't think of anything to write, except "guaca",' he explained.

'That's why we are here,' Eva answered. 'To find out more information.'

Eva was always so calm.[8] He felt good sitting next to her.

'I think we should start with the Kogi,' she continued. 'Yesterday Mr Parra explained that the Kogi are a tribe of people who live in the Sierra Nevada and that their ancestors[9] made a lot of the gold *guaca* that is now in museums around the world.'

Eva typed 'Kogi' and pressed 'enter'. Lucho looked hard at the computer screen, but he really wanted to look at Eva. Soon Eva had found the web page she was looking for.

'OK.' Eva started reading. 'The Sierra Nevada mountains are home to the Kogi tribe. The ancestors of the Kogi were the brave Tairona, who fought for many, many years against the Spanish,' she continued. 'Like their ancestors, the Kogi still make things from gold.'

'Should I write this down?' asked Lucho.

'Of course, or we will forget it,' Eva answered.

Lucho took his notebook and a pen out of his bag. Eva continued reading.

'The Kogi,' she said, 'believe that the jaguar looks after the sun and that the sun gives life to everything. The Kogi name for a jaguar is *Nebtashi*.'

Lucho put his notebook on the table next to the computer and looked at the screen, where there was a photograph of a Kogi chief.[10] The chief was wearing a jaguar skin[11] and he had jaguar teeth on a piece of gold string round his neck. He seemed to be looking straight at Lucho from the screen. Lucho remembered the pendant in his pocket. The jaguar looked out

from the pendant in the same way. Maybe he should show Eva the pendant.

'What are you waiting for, Lucho? Write these things on your mind map!' Eva said.

It was the first time Eva had said his name. It sounded good when she said it. He opened his notebook and turned to the page where he had drawn his mind map, but when he saw what had happened, he almost fell off his chair.

'Eva, something's wrong!' Lucho shouted.

'Shh!' said Eva. 'We're in the library!'

'The mind map has changed, Eva. Look!'

He showed her the mind map. There were words now in the four circles he had drawn with the pendant. The words were, 'Nebtashi', 'Hotel Continental', 'Esmeralda' and 'Ichua'.

'I don't even write like that, Eva!'

'Lucho,' said Eva, 'this is not the time for silly jokes. We don't have much time before the next class.'

'Eva, I promise. All I did last night was to draw the circles and the lines and write "guaca" in the centre circle. Something amazing has happened!'

Eva stood up.

'I'm sorry, Lucho.' Her voice was very serious now. 'I don't think you're a bad person, but you are a little strange. I will do the mind map alone. You can tell your story to Mr Parra on Monday.'

Eva walked out of the library. Lucho didn't know what to think. How had the words appeared on the mind map? Something strange, something very strange, was happening.

Quickly, he typed 'Ichua' into the computer, but couldn't find any information. He now knew that 'Nebtashi' meant 'jaguar', and 'Esmeralda' was his grandmother's name. He looked for information about the 'Hotel Continental', but could only find pages about hotels in places he had never heard of.

'I must show Eva that I'm not lying!' he said to himself as he put his notebook and pen into his bag and stood up. Suddenly he sat down again. Big red letters had started to appear on the computer screen and slowly the letters became words, three words:

'TAKE IT BACK.'

Lucho could not believe his eyes. He had to find Eva!

LOOKING BACK

1 Check your answer to *Looking forward* on page 11.

ACTIVITIES

2 Are the sentences true (*T*) or false (*F*)?
   1 *Arepas* are made of cheese and corn bread. ☐ *T*
   2 Lucho's grandmother used to talk about *guaca*. ☐
   3 There is a yellow bird outside Lucho's bedroom window. ☐
   4 Lucho's grandmother used to work in a hotel. ☐
   5 Lucho draws four circles on his mind map. ☐
   6 Lucho thinks about Eva during English class. ☐
   7 The Tairona made a lot of the *guaca* that is now
      in museums. ☐
   8 Eva leaves the library because the mind map is finished. ☐

3 Match the two parts of the sentences.
   1 Lucho says that he works hard but ☐ *c*
   2 Lucho has got his grandmother's pendant but ☐
   3 Lucho is having a beautiful dream but ☐
   4 Lucho would like to have a haircut but ☐
   5 Lucho looks at his mind map and ☐
   6 Eva doesn't believe Lucho so ☐

   a his mother doesn't know about it.
   b he hasn't got enough time.
   c he doesn't pass his exams.
   d his mother wakes him up.
   e she decides to do the mind map alone.
   f he sees that it has changed.

24

4 <u>Underline</u> the correct words in each sentence.

1 Lucho's mum *knows* / *doesn't know* Eva's mum.

2 Lucho *has* / *hasn't* got a piece of *guaca*.

3 Lucho starts the homework *before* / *after* dinner.

4 In Lucho's dream Lucho and Eva follow a *jaguar* / *bird*.

5 Lucho *likes* / *doesn't like* English.

6 There *is* / *isn't* information on the Internet about the Kogi.

7 *Mr Parra* / *Eva* thinks that Lucho is a little strange.

8 Lucho's *mum's* / *grandmother's* name is Esmeralda.

5 Answer the questions.

1 What did Lucho's grandmother tell Lucho before she died?

2 Where does Lucho keep the pendant?

3 What animal would Lucho like to be?

4 What message appears on the computer screen?

LOOKING FORWARD

6 What do you think? Answer the questions.

1 In Chapter 4, Eva gets a message. What does it say?

2 In Chapter 5, Lucho and Eva go to a shop that sells old things. What do they do there?

Chapter 4

Take it back

Eva was sitting on the grass with her back to the library, reading her history textbook. Lucho tried to walk slowly and calmly towards her, but his legs carried him quickly. Out of the corner of his eye, he could see the little yellow bird flying from one tree to another.

'Eva,' he said softly.

Eva turned and looked at him. She was angry.

'What?' answered Eva. Her voice was cold.

'You have to believe me, Eva. Something strange is happening. When I was at the computer just now, the words "Take it back" appeared.'

'Take what back?' asked Eva. 'What are you talking about?'

'It's time to show her the pendant,' thought Lucho. His grandmother had told him that one day the pendant would ask him to take it back to its home. Eva could help him. He put his hand in his pocket and brought out the blue bag.

'Look,' he said. 'I have never shown this to anybody.'

'What is it?' asked Eva.

'It's a pendant. I think it might be *guaca*,' he answered.

Lucho gave the blue bag to Eva. She opened it and carefully took out the pendant.

'Isn't it beautiful?' asked Lucho.

'It's very beautiful,' Eva said quietly.

'My grandmother gave it to me,' he explained. 'She said I had to look after it, but that one day it would ask me to take it home. I used it to draw the mind map yesterday. I couldn't think what to write in the circles, so I stopped. When I opened my notebook in the library, I saw those words for the first time. I'm telling the truth. I promise, Eva.'

Eva put the pendant back into the blue bag and gave it back to Lucho.

'My grandmother's name was Esmeralda,' continued Lucho. 'She worked in a hotel here in Santa Marta. When she was working at the hotel, an American man gave her the pendant to take care of while he went to Bogota. The man never returned. I don't know the name of the hotel, but maybe it was the Hotel Continental. I tried to find some information about it on the Internet, but I couldn't.'

Eva's phone beeped loudly and they both jumped. She had received a message.

'What's wrong?' asked Lucho.

'The message,' she said slowly. 'It says: "Take it back".'

'The same message as the one on the computer screen!' said Lucho slowly.

'Eva, I'm not sure, but I think the pendant is asking us to help it. I think it's asking us to take it home.'

'But that's impossible,' said Eva. 'That would be magic.'

Lucho didn't know what to say. So many strange things had happened since he had seen the little yellow bird outside the history class window. And now the same message had appeared on the computer screen and on Eva's phone. Eva was right. It *was* like magic.

'Eva,' he said, 'will you help me?'

Eva looked at him. He could see in her eyes that she was afraid.

'I think the pendant has been waiting until there was somebody to help me, Eva. I think it has been waiting for you.'

Eva was thinking hard. She looked past Lucho. He turned and saw that she was looking at a little yellow bird which had landed on the grass behind him.

'I've seen this bird a lot recently,' he said. 'Maybe it's trying to help me.'

Eva corrected him, 'Maybe it's trying to help us, Lucho.'

Lucho smiled.

'Come on,' he said. 'Let's follow it.'

Lucho pulled Eva up by the hand and they followed the little bird over the grass, towards the door to the school building. When they reached the door, Mr Parra, the History teacher, was walking out of the building.

'How is your mind map going, you two?' Mr Parra asked.

Lucho was not sure what to say. They couldn't tell Mr Parra that the mind map seemed to be alive.

'It's going well, sir,' said Eva, 'but we've got a question to ask you. Do you know what "Ichua" means?'

Mr Parra smiled.

'*Ichua* is the name of the most important place in the world for the Kogi,' he explained. 'Their most important chiefs are buried[12] there. The Kogi say it is a secret underground place full of gold, but historians don't believe that it's a real place. I see you have spent your time well in the library.'

It was Lucho's turn to ask a question. 'Mr Parra, do you know if there is a hotel in Santa Marta called the Hotel Continental?'

'Why?' Mr Parra was laughing. 'Are you planning a holiday?'

'No, sir,' answered Lucho, feeling a little stupid.

'Well, there was a hotel called the Hotel Continental in Santa Marta, near the port. But it closed a few years ago,' Mr Parra explained.

Eva watched the little yellow bird fly up to the roof of the library.

'Any more questions?' Mr Parra asked.

'Yes,' said Eva. 'Are birds important in Kogi stories?'

'Oh yes, Eva. There is a bird in every Kogi story. A bird brings a message to the jaguar or it helps the jaguar in its work.

The jaguar, of course, is the most important animal for the Kogi and for many other tribes. The jaguar looks after the Kogi. Without the help of the jaguar, the Kogi believe, the sun would not rise, plants would not grow and rain would not fall.'

Mr Parra smiled.

'I must say I am very pleased that you have been working so well. Don't forget to put all the information on your mind map and bring it to class on Monday.'

Eva and Lucho watched Mr Parra as he walked away from the school building. Lucho's head was full of questions. Had he dreamed that the mind map had grown? Had he added new words in his sleep? But then, why had the message 'TAKE IT BACK' appeared on the computer screen and on Eva's mobile phone? What did the pendant want? Did he have to take it back to *Ichua*? But how could he? Mr Parra had said that *Ichua* probably wasn't a real place.

Lucho followed Eva into the maths classroom. Eva sat next to her best friend and Lucho sat next to Pablo Silva, who was reading a magazine about cars. Lucho said hello to Pablo and opened his notebook. The mind map had grown again! Three new circles had appeared. In the first was a name, 'Mario'. In the second there was another name, 'Salvador'. And in the third was an address, '25 Bastidas Street'.

Pablo stopped reading his car magazine and looked over at Lucho's mind map.

'Is that your mind map for Mr Parra?' Pablo asked. 'Let me see.'

'It's nothing,' Lucho replied and closed his notebook quickly.

When class finally ended, Lucho went straight to Eva's desk.

'I have to show you the mind map,' he said.

Eva asked her friend to wait for her outside the classroom. Lucho opened his notebook.

'It's grown again. Look.'

Eva read the words in the new circles in the mind map, 'Mario', 'Salvador' and '25 Bastidas Street'.

'You see Eva, it's not my handwriting,' Lucho explained.

'I've been thinking, Lucho. Is this Pablo's handwriting?' she asked. 'You were sitting next to him.'

'Of course it isn't. Why would I tell you such a stupid story, Eva?'

'Because you want me to like you,' she replied calmly.

'Eva.' Lucho's voice was strong now. 'If I just wanted you to like me, would I do something like this? Something that makes me look crazy?'

Eva shook her head.

'Of course not,' he continued. 'I'm going to 25 Bastidas Street tomorrow morning, with or without you. I want to know who Salvador and Mario are and I want to know what is happening. Do you want to come with me, or not?'

Lucho couldn't believe that he was talking to Eva Villa in this way.

'Please, please say you are going to come with me,' he thought.

'I said I would help you, Lucho,' answered Eva. 'And I will, if you promise me that this isn't a joke.'

'I promise, Eva,' he said.

'I believe you,' she replied. 'Let's meet in Bastidas Street tomorrow morning at nine o'clock.'

Chapter 5

The antique shop

Bastidas Street was near the port in Santa Marta. Tourists liked to visit this part of town and so did Lucho. Sometimes, after lunch on Sundays, he and his mother would go there for a walk. He often dreamed of getting on one of the boats that moved sadly from side to side and going on an adventure. Now, at last, he was having an adventure and he discovered that it made his head feel light and his heart beat faster.

When he arrived at Bastidas Street, Eva was waiting for him outside a shop that sold very old things: an antique shop. A blue sign with yellow letters said 'Salvador's Antiques'.

'Hello,' said Eva.

'Hello, Eva,' Lucho replied. 'So, Salvador sells antiques, does he?'

'Yes. Has the mind map changed again?' asked Eva, nervously.

'I don't think so,' he replied. 'Not since yesterday.'

Lucho took his notebook out of his bag and looked at the mind map. The same words appeared as the day before: 'guaca', 'Nebtashi', 'Hotel Continental', 'Esmeralda', 'Ichua', 'Mario', 'Salvador' and '25 Bastidas Street'.

'Lucho,' said Eva. 'Before we go inside, tell me everything you know about the pendant again.'

Lucho saw that there was a café across the street from the antique shop.

'Let's get a drink,' he said.

As they drank their juice, Lucho told Eva again about the American who had given his grandmother the pendant when she was working in a hotel in Santa Marta port.

'I asked my mum last night,' he explained. 'She said that the hotel was called the Hotel Continental.'

'But that doesn't help us really, does it?' said Eva. 'I mean, the hotel is closed. Tell me about your grandmother again.'

'There is not a lot more to tell. When I was a boy and my grandmother was dying,' Lucho explained, 'she gave me the pendant and told me to keep it a secret. She said that I shouldn't show it to anybody. You are the first person I've shown it to.'

Eva was listening carefully to every word Lucho said.

'She said that I had to look after it until the correct moment arrived for the pendant to return home.'

They paid for their drinks and crossed Bastidas Street. When they pushed open the door to Salvador's Antiques, they could hear the sound of a bell. Inside the shop it was quite dark, but Lucho and Eva could see that it was full of things made from gold and other expensive metals and stones.

'Look,' said Lucho.

There was a little yellow bird singing in a cage beside the window. Before Eva could say anything, a young man, five or six years older than Lucho and Eva, appeared from a door at the back of the shop. His face, Lucho thought, was like the Kogi chief's they had seen on the Internet.

'What do you want?' he said.

The young man's voice was unfriendly.

'We wanted to ask someone for help with some work for school,' Lucho said to the young man, politely. 'We need some information about *guaca*.'

'We don't sell *guaca* here. We sell objects made by the Kogi, but not *guaca*. I'm sorry, but I can't help you.'

At that moment the door behind the young man opened and Eva and Lucho saw that there was an office behind the door. An older man, with perfect hair and expensive clothes, came into the room.

'Who are your friends, Mario? Why don't you introduce me?'

'Mario,' thought Lucho, remembering the mind map. He looked at Eva. Eva moved her lips without speaking, 'MARIO.'

'I have no idea who they are,' answered Mario, without looking at Eva or Lucho.

'Try to be friendly sometimes, Mario, just sometimes,' the well-dressed man said as he shook both Eva and Lucho's hands. 'Nice to meet you both. My name is Salvador Lana. Now, how can I help you?'

'We have something to show you,' Eva said.

'What?' asked Lucho quickly.

'A pendant,' said Eva. 'Show him, Lucho.'

'But Eva …' said Lucho.

'Don't be afraid,' said Salvador. 'Nothing will happen to your pendant.'

After a few seconds Lucho took the little blue bag from his pocket and handed it to Salvador. Salvador opened the bag and took out the pendant. His eyes became hard, like metal.

'This is a beautiful pendant. Is it yours?' he said.

'Yes, it's mine,' replied Lucho. 'I have to take it to a place called *Ichua*.'

'Ah, *Ichua*,' Salvador said, as he looked at the pendant carefully. 'Interesting.'

'Mario,' said Salvador, after a few seconds. 'What do you think?'

Salvador gave the pendant to Mario. Lucho felt nervous. Who were these men? And why was he showing them his grandmother's pendant?

'Is it what I think it is, Mario? Is it real?'

For a long time Mario just looked at the pendant without speaking. Finally, he handed it back to Salvador.

'It is real,' said Mario.

Salvador looked very happy.

'My friends,' said Salvador, 'I'm sorry, I don't know your names.'

'I'm Lucho, Lucho Valdez. My friend's name is Eva. Eva Villa.' Lucho tried to sound older than he was.

'Well, Lucho Valdez and Eva Villa,' continued Salvador. 'Today is your lucky day.'

Salvador carefully returned the pendant to the little blue bag and gave it back to Lucho.

'You say that you want to take the pendant to *Ichua*,' said Salvador.

'Yes,' replied Lucho. 'It is very important.'

'Well, I can take you to *Ichua* now, if you like. We can be there in a couple of hours.'

'But is *Ichua* a real place?' Eva asked.

'Of course it is, my young friend,' replied Salvador. 'Isn't it, Mario?'

Lucho looked at Mario. Mario, thought Lucho, looked very nervous.

'Some people say it is,' replied Mario.

'Of course it is!' Salvador said. 'That will be all, thank you, Mario. Please go back to work now.'

Mario went through the door behind the counter into the back of the shop. When he closed the door, the little yellow bird stopped singing.

'Is it far?' Lucho asked Salvador.

'Not really. The roads up to the Sierra Nevada are much better than they used to be. Don't worry. We'll be back before dinner.'

Lucho and Eva looked at each other. They both felt nervous.

'OK. Let's go,' said Lucho, as he put the blue bag back into his trouser pocket.

LOOKING BACK

1 Check your answers to *Looking forward* on page 25.

ACTIVITIES

2 Put the sentences in the correct order.
1 Lucho and Eva meet Mario and Salvador in a shop. ☐
2 Mr Parra says that the jaguar looks after the Kogi. ☐
3 Lucho shows Eva the pendant and tells her his story. ☐1
4 The mind map changes again. ☐
5 Eva receives the message, 'Take it back.' ☐
6 Mr Parra explains that *Ichua* is an important place for the Kogi. ☐
7 Mario confirms that the pendant is real. ☐
8 Salvador offers to take Lucho and Eva to *Ichua*. ☐

3 Are the sentences true (*T*) or false (*F*)?
1 Lucho thinks that the pendant is asking for help. ☐T
2 Lucho and Eva think that the yellow bird is trying to help. ☐
3 The Hotel Continental isn't there anymore. ☐
4 In Kogi stories, a jaguar helps a bird in its work. ☐
5 There's an address on the mind map. ☐
6 Lucho shows Pablo his mind map. ☐
7 Lucho has never been to the port. ☐
8 Lucho and Eva have a drink before they go into the shop. ☐
9 Eva shows the pendant to Salvador. ☐
10 Lucho and Eva aren't going to go to *Ichua* with Salvador. ☐

4 What do the underlined words refer to in these lines from the text?

1 'Maybe it's trying to help us, Lucho.' (page 29)
   Lucho and Eva

2 'I am very pleased you have been working so well.' (page 30)
   ....

3 'You were sitting next to him.' (page 32) ....

4 He and his mother would go there for a walk. (page 34)
   ....

5 'She said that the hotel was called Hotel Continental.' (page 35) ....

6 'I have no idea who they are.' (page 37) ....

7 'This is a beautiful pendant. Is it yours?' he said. (page 37)
   ....

8 'It is real,' said Mario. (page 38) ....

5 Answer the questions.

1 What is *Ichua*?
   ....

2 What is the new information on the mind map?
   ....

3 What can you buy in Salvador's Antiques?
   ....

LOOKING FORWARD

• •

6 Tick (✓) what you think happens in the next two chapters.
1 Salvador doesn't take Lucho and Eva to *Ichua*. ☐
2 Salvador takes Lucho and Eva to *Ichua*. ☐

Chapter 6

The jungle is full of surprises

It was the busiest time of day in Santa Marta: the shops had just opened for Saturday morning shoppers and people were driving to their favourite café for breakfast. Salvador's car moved slowly through the busy traffic. Lucho was sitting in the front, next to Salvador, Eva was in the back.

'Would you mind telling us everything you know about *guaca*, Salvador?' Lucho asked. 'Our history teacher says that a lot of *guaca* was taken out of Colombia by foreigners. Is that true?'

Lucho looked at Eva in the mirror and smiled at her. She smiled back and asked him for his notebook and a pen. Lucho handed them to her.

'The story of Colombian *guaca* is very interesting, Lucho,' answered Salvador, 'but very long. I'll tell you everything I know when we get back to the shop.'

For a moment his voice was hard, like his eyes had been when he first saw the pendant. Then it became sweet again.

'You won't be able to write in the car, you see. Just enjoy the journey. Once we get out of Santa Marta and into the Sierra Nevada, it's really beautiful.'

Lucho saw Eva looking at him in the mirror. She had found a page of the notebook where Lucho had written his name and Eva's name in a big heart. She showed it to Lucho. His face turned red.

'Who is Mario?' asked Eva.

'Oh, Mario. I'm sorry about what happened in my shop. Sometimes he's not very friendly,' explained Salvador. 'I asked him to work for me because his ancestors were Kogi goldsmiths, you know, people who make things from gold. In fact, he's the grandson of a Kogi chief. He knows a piece of real *guaca* when he sees it and often he knows where it came from. You see, I always take *guaca* back to the place it came from. I think it's important for Colombia, don't you? All the *guaca* that was made in Colombia should come back home.'

Lucho felt happy because he was taking the pendant back to its home – just as Lucho's grandmother had asked him to do.

The road was going up now into the Sierra Nevada mountains. As they climbed through the fog, Salvador explained how the vegetation changed from banana trees, to corn and pumpkin[13] plants, coffee and sugar plants and finally to potatoes and onions. Each plant, Salvador explained, was planted where it would grow best.

'The Kogi look after the mountains and they know the mountain jungle better than anyone,' said Salvador. 'We might meet some Kogi people along the way.'

Lucho looked out at the thick vegetation all round them. Suddenly he saw the little yellow bird.

'Did you see that, Eva?'

'See what?' she asked.

'The little yellow bird from school. Look, there it is again. It's following us.'

Eva looked out the window and saw the bird. It did look like the same bird they had seen at school and in the antique shop. Salvador saw it too. He seemed nervous.

'The jungle is full of surprises,' said Salvador. 'Now, tell me about the pendant. Where did you get it?'

'My grandmother gave it to me. She worked in the Hotel Continental.'

'Really?' said Salvador.

'An American gave it to her to look after,' Lucho continued, 'but he never came back for it. My grandmother said I should look after it. She told me that one day it would ask to go home.'

Lucho wanted to talk to Eva about the decision to show Salvador the pendant, but there had been no time. Maybe everything was OK: the pendant had told them how to find the way to Salvador's antique shop and now they were going to *Ichua*; but Lucho did not feel comfortable with Salvador for some reason.

A few minutes later the air became cold and a storm started. Within two minutes the road had become a river and the rain fell so heavily that they could hardly see through the car windows. Suddenly the car stopped.

'The wheels won't move,' Salvador said. 'When the rain stops, I'll have to ask you both to get out and help me push.'

'When will the rain stop?' asked Eva.

'Soon. The rain comes and goes quickly in March.'

Salvador was right. Five minutes later the sky was bright again and they got out of the car.

'Let's walk a little first,' said Salvador. 'It's not good for your legs to sit down for so long.'

Lucho and Eva started walking behind Salvador. Lucho saw the little yellow bird fly over the road and behind them. He pointed to it and said, 'Look, Eva. The little yellow bird again. I'm sure it's the same one.'

Eva and Lucho turned to look at the bird, then turned back to follow Salvador. But Salvador had stopped walking and was pointing a gun at them.

'I am very sorry,' he said, 'but I'm afraid I must ask you to walk towards me slowly, my young friend, with the pendant in your right hand.'

The yellow bird flew behind Salvador and disappeared behind a tree. Lucho tried to think. He couldn't give the pendant to Salvador. His grandmother had told him to look after it. If he gave the pendant to Salvador, he was sure Salvador would sell it.

'You see, I've been looking for your pendant all my life,' said Salvador. 'I will look after it now. Please, come forward.'

Lucho didn't move. He would never give the pendant to Salvador. He would never break his promise to his grandmother.

'Tell your boyfriend, young lady,' said Salvador as he pointed the gun at Eva, 'that if he doesn't give me the pendant, I will shoot you. And then I will shoot him.' Then Salvador put his finger on the trigger.

Chapter 7

Nebtashi

'I won't ask you again,' Salvador told Lucho.

'Give it to him, Lucho,' said Eva. 'If you don't, he'll kill us!'

'Listen to her, Lucho,' said Salvador.

Salvador was serious.

'Give me the pendant now, Lucho, or I'll take it from you when you're both too dead to stop me.'

A noise came from behind the tree where the yellow bird had disappeared. Salvador turned to see what it was, but there was nothing to see.

'Why do you want it?' asked Lucho.

'You ask too many questions, my young friend,' replied Salvador.

Again a noise came from behind the tree. Again Salvador turned to look. Suddenly Lucho felt that his legs had become amazingly strong. Without thinking he jumped forward and flew through the air like a cat, like a jaguar, towards Salvador and landed on Salvador's chest. He saw the gun fly into the air. As Salvador fell to the ground, Lucho felt Salvador's head hit the jungle floor.

Before either Lucho or Eva could move, Mario appeared from behind the tree where the little bird had been, picked up the gun and pointed it at Salvador. Everything was real, but it felt like a dream.

'There's a rope in the back of the car,' said Mario quickly. 'Get it. We need to tie Salvador up. He's a dangerous man.'

'Why should we believe you?' Eva asked. 'You work for Salvador.'

'The jaguar pendant your grandmother gave you should be in the tomb of my great-grandfather,[14]' Mario said, all the time pointing the gun at Salvador. 'I have been working for Salvador for three years now. He pays me to find real *guaca* and then he sells it to collectors for lots of money. I helped him, but only because I was waiting for the pendant to return. The Kogi will never be great again, like their ancestors the Tairona, until the pendant is back where it should be. Now, get the rope, before he wakes up!'

Mario kept the gun pointed at Salvador while Eva and Lucho took the rope from the car and used it to tie Salvador's hands and feet.

'What should we do with him?' asked Eva when they had finished.

'Help me move him to the side of the road,' answered Mario. 'Someone will find him.'

They moved Salvador and got back into the car. Mario started the engine, turned the car round and drove down the mountain.

'Where are we going?' asked Lucho.

'To my village. They are waiting for us.'

'Who is waiting for us?' asked Eva.

'The Kogi, of course,' replied Mario.

The jungle flew past them as they raced down the wet mountain road.

'How did you find us in the jungle, Mario?' asked Lucho.

'I didn't find you, I followed you.'

Lucho thought for a moment.

'So where is your car?' he asked.

'There's no time for questions now,' answered Mario. 'Please check that the pendant is OK.'

Lucho took the blue bag from his trouser pocket and opened it. He held the pendant to the sun. The bird and the jaguar's head shone.

'Tell us about the pendant, Mario,' said Eva.

'The pendant was taken from *Ichua* and now it is ready to go back home,' replied Mario. 'The jaguar and the little bird must take it there.'

'The jaguar and the little bird?' asked Lucho. 'Like the ones on the pendant?'

Mario smiled. 'Yes, Lucho. I will help you to take the pendant back to *Ichua*, to my great-grandfather's grave.[15] You must be brave.'

Lucho saw in the mirror that Eva was looking at him.

'I will try my best,' said Lucho.

They drove quickly down the dangerous mountain road and then Mario stopped the car. When they got out, Eva gave Lucho her hand, just like in his dream. Then they followed Mario into the jungle. Lucho could feel his heart beating faster than ever as he held Eva's hand in his. They walked along paths[16] that were more than a thousand years old. Strange animal noises came from the left and the right of them. Beautiful birds flew from tree to tree.

'Where do the people live, Mario?' asked Eva.

'You will see,' he answered.

They crossed bridges over beautiful rivers and saw trees as tall as many of the buildings in Santa Marta.

'The jungle smells of new life after the storm,' said Eva.

Lucho agreed. He felt happy and afraid at the same time. He and Eva were still holding hands. The truth was that holding hands was not a good idea when trying to walk through the jungle, but Lucho did not want to take his hand from Eva's and, it seemed, she didn't want to take her hand from his. They walked on. Their legs were tired and the ground under their feet was wet and dangerous, but Mario did not slow down.

'How do you feel, Eva?' asked Lucho.

'I'm hungry,' she answered.

'The jungle is full of food,' said Mario. 'Wait here.'

Mario disappeared into the jungle. While he was gone, Lucho expected Eva to take her hand back, but she didn't. Mario returned with two pieces of fruit, which he opened and gave to Lucho and Eva. The fruit tasted sweet and was delicious. Mario smiled when he saw that Lucho and Eva were enjoying the food he had brought for them.

'What are they?' asked Eva.

'They are called cherimoya,' said Mario. 'They're delicious, aren't they?'

Eva and Lucho agreed.

'Listen,' said Mario.

Lucho and Eva stopped eating and listened. They could hear the sound of voices, maybe hundreds of them. They were whispering the word 'Nebtashi.'

'They're waiting,' said Mario seriously.

'How do they know we're coming?' asked Eva.

'They know many things,' Mario replied.

As they walked on, the sound of the word 'Nebtashi' grew louder. Finally, when they were almost too tired to walk any more, the path turned a corner and there, in front of them, they saw a village.

'Look,' said Eva. 'Look, Lucho, the Kogi!'

Maybe a thousand Kogi people were standing round a fire that had been lit in the centre of the village. It was clear that nobody had lived in the village for a long time. The men were carrying spears; the women were wearing beautiful clothes. Mario walked forward, followed by Eva and Lucho, and everybody stopped whispering. The jungle was almost silent.

'Is this *Ichua*?' Eva asked Mario, quietly.

'No, but *Ichua* is not far now,' he replied.

They followed Mario as he walked through the sea of

people to a house in the centre of the village. Then they stood a few metres in front of the door to the house and waited. After a few moments an old man came out of the house. The old man was wearing a jaguar skin like a coat, and teeth round his neck and black circles painted on his face and chest. Lucho remembered the photo of the Kogi chief they had seen on the Internet. Was this the same man many years later?

'My grandfather, the chief,' said Mario.

Mario walked towards the old man and said a few words in a language Lucho and Eva couldn't understand. The old man seemed to be asking Mario lots of questions.

Mario returned to Lucho and Eva.

'The chief wants to see the pendant,' said Mario. 'Lucho, he wants you to go inside.'

The chief turned and entered the circular house and Lucho and Mario started to follow him. Nervously, Lucho looked back at Eva. Two Kogi men had brought a chair for her to sit on and some women were offering her food.

'Don't worry,' said Mario. 'The Kogi know why you are both here. My people will look after Eva.'

LOOKING BACK

1 Check your answer to *Looking forward* on page 41.

ACTIVITIES

2 Are the sentences true (*T*) or false (*F*)?
1 Salvador tells Lucho the story of *guaca*. ☐ F
2 Mario has Kogi ancestors. ☐
3 The yellow bird follows Lucho and Eva. ☐
4 Salvador wants Lucho's pendant. ☐
5 Mario saves Eva from Salvador. ☐
6 Mario has been waiting for Lucho's pendant to return. ☐
7 Mario ties Salvador up. ☐
8 Mario says that he has driven into the jungle. ☐

3 Complete the sentences with the names in the box.

> The Kogi   The Kogi chief   Mario
> ~~Mario's grandfather~~   Salvador

1 _Mario's grandfather_ is a Kogi chief.

2 .... sells *guaca* to collectors.

3 .... need the pendant to be great again.

4 .... finds fruit for Eva and Lucho.

5 .... is wearing a jaguar skin.

4 <u>Underline</u> the correct words in each sentence.

1 It was a bad time to drive in Santa Marta because everyone was going *to work / shopping*.

2 Mario recognises *guaca* because he's a *goldsmith / Kogi*.

3 The car stops in the *storm / fog*.

4 Salvador is going to shoot *Lucho / Eva* first.

5 *Mario / Lucho* jumps on Salvador.

6 Lucho and Eva *have something / don't have anything* to eat in the jungle.

7 The Kogi *don't know / know* that Lucho and Eva are coming.

5 Answer the questions.

1 Why does Salvador really want Lucho and Eva to walk a little?

....

2 How is Lucho similar to a jaguar in Chapter 7?

....

3 Why is the pendant important for Mario?

....

4 Describe the Kogi chief.

....

LOOKING FORWARD

• •

6 Tick (✓) what you think happens in the next two chapters.

1 Eva has a problem. ☐

2 Lucho returns the pendant to *Ichua*. ☐

3 Salvador comes back. ☐

Chapter 8

The chief

The chief sat opposite the door, looking into the small fire that was in the centre of the room and, with a movement of his head, showed Lucho where to sit. Then he closed his eyes and began speaking. Mario, who was listening carefully to his grandfather's words, did not speak.

The chief became silent and looked into the fire. Lucho did the same. For a moment, he thought he could see Eva and a bird and a jaguar in the fire, just like in the dream he had at the start of his adventure. The chief stood up, walked slowly across the dirt floor, and put his hands together in front of Lucho. Lucho understood. He took the little blue bag from his pocket and put it in the chief's hands.

The chief took the pendant out of the bag and looked at it for a long time. Then he gave it back to Lucho and began to speak again. This time, Mario translated the chief's words.

'He says your grandmother came here once. He says her name was Esmeralda. He says that she wanted to give the pendant back to the Kogi, but it was not the right moment. He says that the jaguar always waits for the right moment.'

'Gran had been up here in the jungle!' thought Lucho. 'How on earth had she found the village?'

'The chief says that you must take the pendant back to *Ichua*,' said Mario. 'He says that you must go with me and your girlfriend. He says that *Nebtashi* will look after you.'

Lucho smiled. Eva Villa, his girlfriend? Maybe she was his girlfriend now. That sounded good to him!

The chief picked up a small bowl full of water and threw

the water on the fire in the centre of the room. Purple smoke came from the fire.

'Take your shirt off, Lucho,' Mario translated.

The chief put his left hand into the place where the hot fire had been and held it there for a second.

'Stand up, Lucho,' Mario said.

Lucho stood in front of the chief for a while. The chief drew circles all over Lucho's chest, back and face with a burnt stick from the fire.

'He says that you're now one of the jaguar's people, Lucho,' Mario translated. 'He says the moment has come. He says you are a good person. We must go.'

Mario and Lucho followed the chief outside. Eva was sitting next to a young Kogi man with a spear. When the Kogi people saw Lucho, Mario and the chief, they started whispering the word 'Nebtashi' again. Eva stood up and walked towards Lucho.

'You look like a jaguar,' she said. 'You look quite handsome in fact!'

This time Lucho did not turn red. He touched her face and said, 'Thank you.' This time it was Eva who turned red.

'We must go,' said Mario. 'Give me the pendant please, Lucho.'

Lucho gave Mario the little blue bag. When he took it out of his pocket, the Kogi people made a strange noise like a jaguar. Then the Kogi were silent.

Lucho and Eva followed Mario into the jungle. Mario held the pendant in front of him.

'I think he's using the pendant to find the way,' said Eva.

'We must climb,' said Mario.

They climbed through the dark mountain jungle for a very long time until the air became so thin that they felt tired. Soon there was no path and Mario had to use a knife his grandfather had given him to cut a way through the jungle. Spiders fell on their heads and plants near the ground cut their legs. Living in the jungle couldn't be easy, Lucho decided.

'We are close now,' said Mario.

'I hope so,' said Eva, 'I have never felt so tired in my life.'

The pendant was turning in Mario's hand. Lucho looked at it. Questions began to fill his mind. How was it possible that this small piece of gold was telling them the way to go and why had the pendant chosen him and Eva to help it get back home? But it was too late to ask questions like these now. Mario had cut down the plant that was in front of them and they could see light coming through the dark trees around them.

'*Ichua*,' Mario whispered.

Lucho and Eva walked on until they were standing beside Mario. In front of them was a circle of short dry yellow grass.

'It looks like a sun, doesn't it, Lucho?' Eva whispered.

'Eva and I must stay outside the circle. Only the person that *Nebtashi* has chosen can enter,' explained Mario.

Lucho looked at the yellow circle in front of him and remembered the last three days: the yellow bird outside the history class, outside his kitchen window, in the antique shop; the dream, the messages in the library and the mind map that had strangely grown and then taken them to Salvador's shop; Salvador, ready to shoot them; the chief, the Kogi village and now the final step. If he ever tried to tell anyone of his adventure, they would think he was mad. Everybody except Eva. Mario gave the pendant back to Lucho and Lucho stepped into the yellow circle.

'You must find the door to *Ichua*.' Mario's voice seemed to come from a dream. 'Move round the circle, Lucho. The pendant will help you.'

'And then what?' asked Lucho.

But it was too late for any more questions. Lucho turned, but everything outside the yellow circle was hidden behind purple smoke.

'Eva!' he shouted. 'Mario! What does the door to *Ichua* look like?'

There was no reply.

Suddenly Lucho felt cold. He looked up into the sky and saw that there was a cloud above him. The cloud looked like a jaguar. When Lucho looked down again, he saw that black circles had appeared on the yellow grass, just like the circles on a jaguar's skin or a mind map!

'That's it,' Lucho shouted. 'The circles on the grass are in exactly the same places as the circles on the mind map. If I can remember which circle of the mind map had the word 'Ichua' written in it, I will be closer to finding the door to *Ichua*!'

With his eyes closed, he tried to remember the mind map. He opened his eyes and walked to the spot he thought was *Ichua*. Then he closed his eyes again. He had to be sure. Again he tried to 'see' the mind map.

He was sure. He stepped onto the black circle he hoped was the door to *Ichua*. Suddenly the ground under his feet disappeared, the black spot had turned into a hole and he fell deep, deep down, into the ground.

Chapter 9

Ichua

When Lucho landed, he found himself in a circular tunnel. The light coming from the pendant in his hand lit the walls and the floor of the tunnel, which were covered in gold. The tunnel was long and went to his left and to his right. He walked to his right and the light coming from the pendant did not change. He walked to his left and there was no change either.

'The pendant isn't showing me which way to go,' he thought.

Then something even more amazing happened: the little yellow bird flew out of the pendant, waited in the air for Lucho to follow it, and then flew off, singing.

The bird was fast and Lucho had to run. When he turned the corner at the end of the first tunnel, he saw that there was another tunnel in front of him. Everything was gold. The light from the pendant lit the walls, the ceiling and the floor and was so strong that Lucho couldn't see. His only hope was to follow the singing of the bird. He turned corner after corner and ran along tunnel after tunnel, until finally he saw a light as bright as the sun, coming from around the next corner.

Lucho slowly turned the corner and the light became less bright. He walked into a circular room covered in gold. In the centre of the room was a big square stone. In the centre of the stone was a hole, about the same size as the pendant.

'Now what do I do?' Lucho asked himself. 'Maybe I should put the pendant into the hole?'

He looked for the little yellow bird for help, but the bird had disappeared. He looked at the pendant, but the pendant just looked like a piece of gold with a jaguar's head and a little yellow bird on it.

'You've got nothing to lose now, Lucho,' he said to himself and then he walked towards the stone and carefully put the pendant into the hole.

'Ahh!' shouted Lucho as he fell to the floor. As soon as the pendant had disappeared inside the stone, everything went black and a noise like an angry jaguar shook the room. Then the floor started moving from side to side and everything seemed to turn and turn. Purple light filled the room and for a moment Lucho thought that he saw his grandmother in front of him.

'Help me out of here, Gran!' Lucho shouted.

'Shh,' said Lucho's grandmother. She put her finger to her lips and disappeared. Then the room stopped shaking, the roaring noise became weaker and then stopped, and the purple light disappeared.

As Lucho climbed to his feet in darkness now, he heard a noise he had heard before: the little yellow bird had returned. It filled the room with the light that came from its wings. Lucho quickly looked around him. The stone in the centre of the room was still there, but the hole in its surface[17] had disappeared. There was no time to think. The bird had already flown out of the room, taking its light with it. He listened for its song and followed.

It was the same tiring game. Lucho turned corner after corner and went along dark tunnel after dark tunnel. He didn't see the bird again and had to listen for its song. He had never felt so tired. He had to return to Eva and Mario, but all he wanted was to stop and rest. Then, when he was so tired he could only move on his hands and knees, he came to some stairs and began to climb.

Lucho climbed the stairs for a long, long time. On every step he stopped and rested. The bird had disappeared, but there was only one way to go: up!

When he was close to losing all hope, Lucho heard Eva's voice.

'Come on, Lucho,' she shouted. 'Come on, you can do it!'

Eva was waiting for him; he couldn't stop now! Eva's voice became closer with every step he climbed. Two hands began to pull him up. Lucho opened his tired eyes. They were Eva's hands!

'Help me, Eva!' he cried.

Eva pulled and pulled and, at last, Lucho was back on the circle of dry yellow grass.

'It's OK, Lucho. Everything is OK,' said Eva. Then she kissed him on the cheek.

Lucho looked down at his body. The black circles that the chief had painted on him had disappeared.

'Look, Lucho, look at the grass circle,' said Eva.

With their mouths open, they watched as new plants grew where before there had been a yellow circle of dry grass. Soon the plants were as tall as the plants around them and the yellow grass circle was just a memory.

'Where's Mario?' asked Lucho.

'He told me to wait for him here, outside the yellow circle,' Eva replied.

'You have done what the jaguar asked you to do, Lucho.'

Mario's voice seemed to come from the sky. He had been in the tree above them and was climbing down.

'Where did you go, Mario?' asked Lucho angrily. 'Why didn't you look after Eva?'

'I asked the jungle to look after her. And it did,' said Mario, as he allowed himself to fall to the jungle floor from the lowest branches of the tree.

He looked straight into Lucho's eyes.

'You were in too much danger down there for me to leave you alone and I think Eva is clever enough to look after herself, don't you?'

Mario and Eva smiled at Lucho.

'Mario looked after me,' Lucho said to himself. 'Was it possible that he was the little yellow bird? Of course it was possible,' he told himself. 'Anything was possible with the jaguar's help.'

'What happened, Lucho?' asked Eva.

'I can't really remember,' answered Lucho.

'He took the pendant back home,' said Mario. 'He was brave, very brave: as brave as a jaguar in fact! Come. It's time to go.'

'What time is it?' asked Eva.

'I can't see the sun here,' answered Mario, 'but it must be about twelve o'clock, the air is very warm.'

'Only twelve o'clock! That's impossible!' said Eva. 'We met at Salvador's shop at nine o'clock.'

'*Nebtashi* makes everything possible,' said Mario. 'Now we must go.'

LOOKING BACK

1 Check your answer to *Looking forward* on page 57.

ACTIVITIES

2 Are the sentences true (*T*) or false (*F*)?
1 Lucho meets the Kogi chief. ☐ *T*
2 Lucho's grandmother never went to the jungle. ☐
3 Mario uses the pendant to find the way to *Ichua*. ☐
4 Lucho's mind map helps him find the door to *Ichua*. ☐
5 *Ichua* is under the ground. ☐
6 The pendant leads Lucho through the tunnels. ☐
7 The light turns purple when Lucho enters the circular room. ☐
8 Lucho asks his grandmother for help. ☐
9 Eva can't believe that it is only 12 o'clock. ☐

3 <u>Underline</u> the correct words in each sentence.
1 The Kogi chief paints *Mario's / <u>Lucho's</u>* body.
2 *Lucho / Mario* translates the Kogi chief's words.
3 Lucho looks like a *yellow bird / jaguar*.
4 Lucho remembers his adventure when he *looks at the yellow circle / listens to the yellow bird*.
5 There *is / isn't* gold in the tunnel.
6 The floor starts moving *after / before* Lucho returns the pendant.
7 Lucho hears *Mario's / Eva's* voice from the tunnel.
8 The yellow circle *disappears / doesn't disappear* after Lucho leaves the tunnel.
9 *The Kogi chief / Mario* was the yellow bird in the tunnel.

4 What do the <u>underlined</u> words refer to in these lines from the text?

1 'You look like a jaguar,' <u>she</u> said. (page 59) .... *Eva*

2 '<u>It</u> looks like a sun, doesn't it, Lucho?' (page 61)

  ....

3 ... waited in the air for Lucho to follow <u>it</u>. (page 64)

  ....

4 '<u>He</u> told me to wait for him here.' (page 68) ....

5 He had been in the tree above <u>them</u>. (page 68)

  ....

6 '<u>He</u> took the pendant back home.' (page 69)

  ....

5 Answer the questions.

1 Why didn't the Kogi accept the pendant when Esmeralda took it back to them?

  ....

2 Why does Lucho decide that it can't be easy to live in the jungle?

  ....

3 How does Lucho find the correct door to *Ichua*?

  ....

4 Where does Lucho leave the pendant?

  ....

LOOKING FORWARD

• •

6 What do you think? Answer the questions.

1 Do Lucho and Eva get home safely?

  ....

2 Do Lucho and Eva tell everyone their story?

  ....

Chapter 10

History class

Mario had been right. They arrived back at Santa Marta at four o'clock on Saturday afternoon and their parents didn't ask too many difficult questions. The jaguar, it seemed, really had stopped time.

Sunday passed really slowly. Lucho tried to concentrate,[18] but could only think of Eva and the adventure they had shared in the Sierra Nevada de Santa Marta.

Finally Monday arrived. Eva was already in history class when Lucho walked in that morning, last as usual. She smiled at Lucho. Pablo Silva saw her smile.

'I see your mind map went well,' said Pablo.

'Not bad,' said Lucho. 'I'm going for a pizza with Eva after school.'

'Really!' said Pablo. 'I didn't think you were brave enough to ask any girl out.'

'I had some help,' answered Lucho.

'OK, quiet, quiet,' said Mr Parra as he came into class. 'I hope you had a good weekend and that you made good progress with your mind maps. I'd like you all to come to the front with your partner and draw your mind map on the board.'

Mr Parra always asked them to do this. He said the best way to write well was to have lots of ideas and to share them.

'Remember,' he continued, 'you can write down in your notebook any ideas that you think are interesting.'

Eva turned to look at Lucho and smiled.

'Well …' said Pablo, 'she really likes you.'

Lucho stepped on Pablo's foot under the desk.

'Be quiet, Pablo,' whispered Lucho, 'I'm trying to listen.'

Pablo looked at his friend in surprise – this was something he had never heard Lucho say before – but decided it was best not to say anything more.

Each student went with their partner to the front of the class and drew their mind maps on the board. Some of them were excellent; some of them were just OK. As usual, everybody had done their homework.

'So,' said Mr Parra, 'the last pair. Eva Villa and Lucho Valdez, please.'

Lucho stood up and walked to the front of the class, where Eva was already waiting for him.

'If I remember correctly,' Mr Parra continued, 'you had a very interesting question about *Ichua*. Did you find any more information about it?'

'We decided that *Ichua* is not a real place, sir,' answered Eva.

'I see.' said Mr Parra. 'OK. Show me what you've done.'

Lucho opened his notebook to the pages where he had drawn his mind map while Eva watched him. Lucho's face turned white.

'What's wrong, Lucho?' she asked.

'It's gone. Look, it's gone!'

The pages where the mind map had been were empty.

'Is this a joke, Lucho?' asked Mr Parra. 'There is a time and a place for jokes and my classroom is not one of them.'

Lucho didn't know what to say. Eva started speaking, but Mr Parra stopped her.

'That's enough!' shouted Mr Parra.

'Mr Parra,' continued Eva. 'We did draw a mind map. It's just that … something strange has happened to it.'

'Strange things only happen in films, Miss Villa,' replied Mr Parra.

Lucho had to think of something quickly. If he didn't, Mr Parra might give them more homework for the next day. That would mean that there wouldn't be enough time to have a pizza with Eva that evening.

'Mr Parra,' Lucho began, 'please believe us. I promise that we did a mind map. If I close my eyes, I can remember it.'

'Well,' said Mr Parra, 'if a mind map is good, we can usually remember it without looking at it.'

'Let me try, Mr Parra,' said Lucho.

'I will give you one chance. But,' Mr Parra stood up and looked at both Eva and Lucho, 'if all you are going to do is to use the words and ideas that your classmates have already written on the blackboard, you will be in serious trouble. Is that understood?'

'Yes, sir,' replied Eva and Lucho.

'Help me please, Eva,' asked Lucho, 'if I forget anything.'

Lucho began drawing. First he drew the centre circle with the word 'guaca' in it, and then he drew two more circles, one above and one below, and drew lines between them and the centre circle. In the top circle he wrote 'Kogi' and in the bottom circle 'collectors'. Mr Parra watched carefully, but did not speak.

Next Lucho drew two circles under 'collectors' and wrote 'good' and 'bad'. In another circle, under 'bad', he wrote 'never return guaca' and in a circle under 'good', he wrote 'return guaca'. Then he went back to the circle that said 'Kogi' and drew three more circles above it. In these he wrote 'Ichua', 'Nebtashi' and 'bird'.

Then he drew a line between 'return guaca' and 'Ichua'.

'Stop, stop,' said Mr Parra. 'Your mind map is obviously going to be big and we only have five minutes until the end of class. You seem to have a good memory, Lucho, but how about you, Eva? Can you tell me anything interesting about *guaca*?'

Lucho could see what she was thinking. If she told Mr Parra and the class what had really happened to them, thanks to their mind map, they would think that she was mad.

'What about the story we heard about the woman who worked at the Hotel Continental?' said Lucho.

'Ah yes,' said Eva. 'We went to an antique shop, sir, and asked the people who worked there some questions. They told us about an American collector who had stayed at the Hotel Continental a few years ago. The American asked one of the ladies who cleaned the rooms to look after a gold pendant with a jaguar's head and a bird on it while he was in Bogota. He said it was *guaca* and that when he returned he was going to take it back to *Ichua*.'

'Go on,' said Mr Parra.

'Unfortunately, the American collector never came back from Bogota and nobody knows what happened to the pendant.'

'What do the people in the shop think happened to it?' asked Mr Parra.

'They think,' answered Lucho, 'that the woman probably sold it to another collector.'

Mr Parra stood up. He had something important to say.

'That's probably true,' said Mr Parra. 'You see, the great problem with *guaca* is that people don't see the real importance of it. Much of it has special meaning to our country, but people only see it as a way to make money. What would you do if you found a piece of *guaca*, Lucho?'

Lucho looked at Eva.

'Eva and I have already talked about this, Mr Parra,' said Lucho. 'We would try to take the *guaca* back to the place it came from.'

'Yes,' said Eva. 'I'm sure it wouldn't be easy, but we would try.'

LOOKING BACK

1 Check your answers to *Looking forward* on page 70.

ACTIVITIES

2 Are the sentences true (*T*) or false (*F*)?
1 Lucho and Eva get home on Saturday morning. ☐F☐
2 Their parents ask them a lot of questions. ☐
3 Lucho gets to school early on Monday. ☐
4 Lucho has asked Eva to go out with him. ☐
5 Eva says that *Ichua* exists. ☐
6 The mind map has disappeared from Lucho's notebook. ☐
7 Mr Parra is worried that Eva and Lucho are going to copy their classmates' ideas. ☐
8 Eva doesn't tell all the truth about the pendant. ☐
9 Mr Parra says that everyone understands the importance of *guaca*. ☐

3 Underline the correct words in each sentence.
1 Lucho and *Pablo / Eva* are going for a pizza after school.
2 The students have to *draw their mind maps / write a summary* on the board.
3 Lucho *is / isn't* interested in the history class today.
4 Lucho says he *can / can't* remember his mind map.
5 Lucho asks *Pablo / Eva* for help.
6 Lucho *finishes / doesn't finish* the mind map.
7 Mr Parra says that *guaca* has a special meaning to *collectors / Colombia*.
8 Eva says that it *would / wouldn't* be difficult to return *guaca* back to its original place.

4 Complete the sentences with the names in the box.

| Mr Parra (x3)   Lucho   Eva (x2)   Pablo |

1 _Eva_ smiles at Lucho in class.
2 .... talks to Lucho at the beginning of the class.
3 .... thinks that it's good to share ideas.
4 .... steps on Pablo's foot.
5 .... wants to know about *Ichua*.
6 .... thinks that Lucho is lying about his mind map.
7 .... tells the story about the antique shop.

5 Match the two parts of the sentences.
1 Pablo is surprised because [c]
2 The mind maps are not all excellent but [ ]
3 Mr Parra is angry with Lucho because [ ]
4 Lucho hasn't got his mind map but [ ]

a he thinks that he hasn't done his homework.
b everybody has done their homework.
c Lucho wants to concentrate in class.
d he can draw it from memory.

6 Answer the questions.
1 What does Mr Parra say is the best way to write well?

....

2 Why does Lucho have to stop drawing his mind map?

....

3 Why doesn't Eva tell the class about her adventure?

....

4 What is the big problem with *guaca* in Colombia?

....

Glossary

• •

[1]**bright** (page 6) *adjective*   having a strong, light colour; full of light

[2]**object** (page 7) *noun*   a thing that you can see or touch but that is not alive

[3]**antique** (page 7) *adjective*   an **object** that is old and beautiful

[4]**tribe** (page 7) *noun*   a group of people who live together, usually a long way from a city, and who still have a traditional way of life

[5]**collector** (page 7) *noun*   a person who collects **objects** because they are beautiful or interesting

[6]**port** (page 14) *noun*   an area of a town that is next to the water, where ships arrive and leave

[7]**spot** (page 17) *noun*   a small round mark that is a different colour to the **surface** it is on

[8]**calm** (page 20) *adjective*   relaxed

[9]**ancestor** (page 20) *noun*   a person in your family who lived a long time ago

[10]**chief** (page 21) *noun*   the most important person in a tribe

[11]**skin** (page 21) *noun*   the outer part of (here) an animal's body

[12]**bury** (page 29) *verb*   to put a dead body into the ground

[13]**pumpkin** (page 43) *noun*   a large round vegetable with thick, orange **skin**

[14]**great-grandfather** (page 49) *noun*   the father of your grandfather

[15]**grave** (page 50) *noun*   a place in the ground where a dead body is **buried**

[16]**path** (page 51) *noun*   a long thin piece of ground for people to walk on

[17]**surface** (page 67) *noun*   the top or outside part of something

[18]**concentrate** (page 72) *verb*   to think very hard about the thing you are doing and nothing else